Edward Bulwer Lytton

Walpole

Or, every man has his price, a comedy in rhyme in three acts

Edward Bulwer Lytton

Walpole
Or, every man has his price, a comedy in rhyme in three acts

ISBN/EAN: 9783744793988

Printed in Europe, USA, Canada, Australia, Japan

Cover: Foto ©Andreas Hilbeck / pixelio.de

More available books at **www.hansebooks.com**

WALPOLE

OR

EVERY MAN HAS HIS PRICE

A COMEDY IN RHYME

IN THREE ACTS

BY

LORD LYTTON

WILLIAM BLACKWOOD & SONS
EDINBURGH AND LONDON
MDCCCLXIX

DRAMATIS PERSONÆ.

THE RIGHT HON. ROBERT WALPOLE, M.P., Chancellor
of the Exchequer, and First Lord of the Treasury.

JOHN VEASEY, M.P., his Confidant.

SELDEN BLOUNT, M.P.

SIR SIDNEY BELLAIR, Bart., M.P.

LORD NITHSDALE.

1ST JACOBITE LORD.

2D JACOBITE LORD.

Frequenters of Tom's Coffee-House, Servants, &c.

WOMEN.

LUCY WILMOT.

MRS VIZARD.

Scene—LONDON, 1716.

Time occupied by the Events of the Play—ONE DAY.

WALPOLE.

———◆———

ACT FIRST.

SCENE I.

Tom's *Coffee-house. In the background, gentlemen
seated in different compartments, or " boxes."*

Enter WALPOLE *and* VEASEY *from opposite sides.*

VEASEY.

Ha! good day, my dear patron.

WALPOLE.

      Good day, my dear friend ;
You can spare me five minutes ?

A

VEASEY.

Five thousand.

WALPOLE.

Attend ;

I am just from the king, and I failed not to press
      him
To secure to his service John Veasey.

VEASEY.

God bless him !

WALPOLE.

George's reign, just begun, your tried worth will
      distinguish.

VEASEY.

Oh, a true English king !

WALPOLE.

Tho' he cannot speak English.

VEASEY.

You must find that defect a misfortune, I fear.

WALPOLE.

The reverse ; for no rivals can get at his ear.
It is something to be the one public man pat in
The new language that now governs England, dog
      Latin.

VEASEY.

Happy thing for these kingdoms that you have that
　　gift,
Or, alas! thro' what shoals all our counsels would
　　drift.

WALPOLE.

Yes, the change from Queen Anne to King George,
　　we must own,
Renders me and the Whigs the sole props of the
　　throne.
For the Tories their Jacobite leanings disgrace,
And a Whig is the only safe man for a place.

VEASEY.

And the Walpoles of Houghton, in all their relations,
Have been Whigs to the backbone for three genera-
　　tions.

WALPOLE.

Ay, my father and mother contrived to produce
Their eighteen sucking Whigs for the family use,
Of which number one only, without due reflection,
Braved the wrath of her house by a Tory connection.
But, by Jove, if her Jacobite husband be living,
I will make him a Whig.

VEASEY.

How ?

WALPOLE.

By something worth giving :
For I loved her in boyhood, that pale pretty sister;
And in counting the Walpoles still left, I have
mist her.

(*Pauses in emotion, but quickly recovers
himself.*)

What *was* it I said ?—Oh,—the State and the
Guelph,
For their safety, must henceforth depend on myself.
The revolt, scarcely quenched, has live sparks in its
ashes ;
Nay, fresh seeds for combustion were sown by its
flashes.
Each example we make dangerous pity bequeathes;
For no Briton likes blood in the air that he breathes.

VEASEY.

Yes; at least there's one rebel whose doom to the
block
Tho' deserved, gives this soft-hearted people a shock.

WALPOLE.

Lord Nithsdale, you mean ; handsome, young, and
    just wedded,—
A poor head, that would do us much harm if
    beheaded.

VEASEY.

Yet they say you rejected all prayers for his life.

WALPOLE.

It is true ; but in private I've talked to his wife :
She had orders to see him last night in the Tower.
And——

VEASEY.

    Well ?

WALPOLE (*looking at his watch*).

Wait for the news—'tis not yet quite the hour.
Ah ! poor England, I fear, at the General Election,
Will vote strong in a mad anti-Whiggish direction.
From a Jacobite Parliament we must defend her,
Or the King will be Stuart, and Guelph the Pretender.
And I know but one measure to rescue our land
From the worst of all ills—Civil War.

VEASEY.
                                    True ; we stand
At that dread turning-point in the life of a State
When its free choice would favour what freedom
    should hate ;
When the popular cause, could we poll popula-
    tion——

WALPOLE.
Would be found the least popular thing in the nation.

VEASEY.
Scarce a fourth of this people are sound in their
    reason——

WALPOLE.
But we can't hang the other three-fourths for high
    treason.

VEASEY.
Tell me, what is the measure your wisdom proposes ?

WALPOLE.
In its third year, by law, this Whig Parliament closes.
But the law ! What's the law in a moment so
    critical ?
Church and State must be saved from a House
    Jacobitical.
Let this Parliament then, under favour of heaven,
Lengthen out its existence from three years to seven.

VEASEY.

Brilliant thought! could the State keep its present
    directors
Undisturbed for a time by those rowdy electors,
While this new German tree, just transplanted,
    takes root,
Dropping down on the lap of each friend golden
    fruit,
Britain then would be saved from all chance of
    reaction
To the craft and corruption of Jacobite faction.
But ah! think you the Commons would swallow
    the question?

WALPOLE.

That depends on what pills may assist their digestion.
I could make—see this list—our majority sure,
If by buying two men I could sixty secure;
For as each of these two is the chief of a section
That will vote black or white at its leader's direction,
Let the pipe of the shepherd but lure the bell-
    wether,
And he folds the whole flock, wool and cry, alto-
    gether.
Well, the first of these two worthy members you guess.

VEASEY.

Sure, you cannot mean Blount, virtuous Selden
    Blount?

WALPOLF.

                       Yes.

VEASEY.

What! your sternest opponent, half Cato, half Brutus,
He, whose vote incorruptible——

WALPOLE.

                Just now would suit us;
For a patriot so stanch could with dauntless
    effrontery——

VEASEY.

Sell himself?

WALPOLE.

    Why, of course, for the good of his country.
True, his price will be high—he is worth forty votes,
And his salary must pay for the change in their
    coats.
Prithee, has not his zeal for his fatherland—rather
Overburthened the lands he received from his
    father?

VEASEY.

Well, 'tis whispered in clubs that his debts some-
    what tease him.

WALPOLE.

I must see him in private, and study to ease him.
Will you kindly arrange that he call upon me
At my home, not my office, to-day—just at three ?
Not a word that can hint at the object in view—
Say some bill in the House that concerns him and
    you ;
And on which, as distinct from all party disputes,
Members meet without tearing each other like
    brutes.

VEASEY.

Lucky thought—Blount and I both agree in Com-
    mittee
On a bill for amending the dues of the City——

WALPOLE.

And the Government wants to enlighten its soul
On the price which the public should pay for its coal.
We shall have him, this Puritan chief of my foes.
Now the next one to catch is the chief of the Beaux ;

All our young members mimic his nod or his laugh;
And if Blount be worth forty votes, he is worth
half.

VEASEY.

Eh ! Bellair, whose defence of the Jacobite
peers——

WALPOLE.

Thrilled the House ; Mister Speaker himself was in
tears.
Faith, I thought he'd have beat us. (*Taking snuff.*)

VEASEY.

That fierce peroration——

WALPOLE.

Which compared me to Nero—superb (*brushing the
snuff from his lace lappet*) declamation !

VEASEY.

Yes ; a very fine speaker.

WALPOLE.

Of that there's no doubt,
For he speaks about things he knows nothing about.

But I still to our party intend to unite him—
Secret Service Department—Bellair—a small item.

VEASEY.

Nay, you jest—-for this gay maiden knight in debate,
To a promise so brilliant adds fortune so great——

WALPOLE.

That he is not a man to be bought by hard cash ;
But he's vain and conceited, light-hearted and rash.
Every favourite of fortune hopes still to be greater,
And a beau must want something to turn a debater.
Hem! I know a Duke's daughter, young, sprightly,
    and fair ;
She will wed as I wish her ; hint that to Bellair ;
Ay, and if he will put himself under my steerage,
Say that with the Duke's daughter I throw in
    the peerage.

VEASEY.

Those are baits that a vain man of wit may seduce.

WALPOLE.

Or, if not, his political creed must be loose ;
To some Jacobite plot he will not be a stranger,
And to win him securely——

VEASEY.

We'll get him in danger.

Hist !

Enter BELLAIR, *humming a tune.*

———

SCENE II.

WALPOLE, VEASEY, BELLAIR.

WALPOLE.

Good morning, Sir Sidney ; your speech did
    you credit ;
And whatever your party, in time you will head it.
Your attack on myself was exceedingly striking,
Tho' the subject you chose was not quite to my
    liking.
Tut I I never bear malice.   You hunt ?

BELLAIR.

Yes, of late.

WALPOLE.

And you ride as you speak ?

BELLAIR.

Well, in both a light weight.

WALPOLE.

But light weights have the odds in their favour, I
fear.
Come and hunt with my harriers at Houghton this
year ;
I can show you some sport.

BELLAIR.

Sir, there's no doubt of that.

WALPOLE.

We will turn out a fox.

BELLAIR (*aside*).

As a bait for a rat !

WALPOLE.

I expect you, next autumn ! Agreed then : good day.
(*Exit* WALPOLE.)

SCENE III.

VEASEY, BELLAIR.

BELLAIR.

Well, I don't know a pleasanter man in his way;
'Tis no wonder his friends are so fond of their chief.

VEASEY.

That you are not among them is matter for grief.
Ah, a man of such stake in the land as yourself,
Could command any post in the Court of the
　　Guelph.

BELLAIR.

No, no; I'm appalled.

VEASEY.

　　By the king? Can you doubt him?

BELLAIR.

I'm appalled by those Gorgons, the ladies about
　　him.

VEASEY.

Good! ha, ha! yes, in beauty his taste may be
　　wrong,
But he has what we want, sir, a government strong.

BELLAIR.

Meaning petticoat government? Mine too is such,
But my rulers don't frighten their subjects so much.

VEASEY.

Nay, your rulers? Why plural? Legitimate sway
Can admit but one ruler to love——

BELLAIR.

And obey.
What a wife! Constitutional monarchy? Well,
If I chose my own sovereign I might not rebel.

VEASEY.

You may choose at your will! With your parts,
    wealth, condition,
You, in marriage, could link all the ends of ambi-
    tion.
There *is* a young beauty—the highest in birth,
And her father, the Duke——

BELLAIR.

Oh, a duke!

VEASEY.

Knows your worth.
Listen : Walpole, desiring to strengthen the Lords
With the very best men whom the country affords,
Has implied to his Grace, that his choice should be
    clear,

(*Carelessly.*)
If you wed the Duke's daughter, of course you're a
    peer.

BELLAIR.

With the Lords and the lady would Walpole ally
    me ?

VEASEY.

Yes ; and, if I were *you*——

BELLAIR.

He would certainly buy me ;
But I,—being a man——
(*Draws himself up haughtily.*)

VEASEY.

No offence.   Why that frown ?

BELLAIR (*relapsing into his habitual ease*).

Nay, forgive me.   Tho' man, I'm a man about
    town;
And so graceful a compliment could not offend
Any man about town, from a Minister's friend.
Still, if not from the frailty of mortals exempt,
Can a mortal be tempted where sins do not tempt?
Of my rank and my fortune I *am* so conceited,
That I don't, with a wife, want those blessings
    repeated.
And tho' flattered to learn I should strengthen
    the Peers—
Give me still our rough House with its laughter
    and cheers.
Let the Lords have their chamber—I grudge not
    its powers;
But for badgering a Minister nothing like ours!
Whisper that to the Minister;—sir, your obedient.
                           (*Turns away.*)

VEASEY (*aside*).

Humph! I see we must hazard the ruder expedient.
If some Jacobite pit for his feet we can dig,
He shall hang as a Tory, or vote as a Whig.
               (VEASEY *retires into the background.*)

B

BELLAIR (*seating himself*).

Oh, how little these formalist middle-aged schemers
Know of *us* the bold youngsters, half sages, half
　　dreamers !
Sages half ?　Yes, because of the time rushing on,
Part and parcel are *we : they* belong to time gone.
Dreamers half ?　Yes, because in a woman's fair face
We imagine the heavën they find in a place.
At this moment I, courted by Whig and by Tory,
For the spangles and tinsel which clothe me with
　　glory,
Am a monster so callous, I should not feel sorrow
If an earthquake engulfed Whig and Tory to-
　　morrow ;
" What a heartless assertion !" the aged would say :
True, the young have no heart, for they give it
　　away.
Ah, I love ! and here—joy !—comes the man who
　　may aid me.

　　　　　　　　　　　　　(*Enter* BLOUNT.)

SCENE IV.

BELLAIR, BLOUNT, VEASEY, ETC.

BLOUNT (*to Coffee-house loungers, who gather round him as he comes down the stage*).

Yes, sir, just from Guildhall, where the City has
    paid me
The great honour I never can merit enough,
Of this box, dedicated to Virtue——

    (*Coffee-house loungers gather round.*)

VEASEY.

                    And snuff.

BLOUNT.

Yes, sir, Higgins the Patriot, who deals in rappee,
Stored that box with pulvillio, superfluous to me ;
For a public man gives his whole life to the nation,
And his nose has no time for a vain titillation.

VEASEY.

On the dues upon coal—apropos of the City—
We agreed——

BLOUNT.

  And were beat ; Walpole bribed the Committee.

VEASEY.

You mistake; he leans tow'rds us, and begs you
    to call
At his house—three o'clock.

BLOUNT (*declaiming as if in Parliament*).

                     But I say, once for all,
That the dues——

VEASEY.

          Put the case as you only can do,
And we carry the question.

BLOUNT.

              I'll call, sir, at two.

VEASEY.

He said three.

BLOUNT.

        I say *two*, sir; my honour's at stake,
To amend every motion that Ministers make.
            (VEASEY *retires into the background.*)

BLOUNT (*advancing to* BELLAIR).

Young debater, your hand. One might tear into
    shreds
All your plea for not cutting off Jacobite heads ;
But that burst against Walpole redeemed your
    whole speech.
Be but honest, and high is the fame you will reach.

BELLAIR.

Blount, your praise would delight, but your cau-
    tion offends.

BLOUNT.

'Tis my way — I'm plain spoken to foes and to
    friends.
What are talents but snares to mislead and pervert
    you,
Unless they converge in one end—Public Virtue !
Fine debaters abound : we applaud and despise
    them ;
For when the House cheers them the Minister buys
    them.
Come, be honest, I say, sir—away with all doubt ;
Public Virtue commands ! Vote the Minister out !

BELLAIR.

Public virtue when construed means private ambition.

BLOUNT.

This to me—to a Patriot——

BELLAIR.

                     In fierce opposition;
But you ask for my vote.

BLOUNT.

            England wants every man.

BELLAIR.

Well, tho' Walpole can't buy me, I think that you
   can.
Blount, I saw you last evening cloaked up to your
   chin;
But I had not a guess who lay, *perdu*, within
All those bales of broadcloth—when a gust of wind
   rose,
And uplifting your beaver it let out your nose.

BLOUNT (*somewhat confusedly*).

Yes, I always am cloaked—half disguised, when I go
Certain rounds—real charity hides itself so ;
For one good deed concealed is worth fifty paraded.

BELLAIR.

Finely said. Quitting, doubtless, the poor you had
    aided,
You shot by me, before I had time to accost you,
Down a court which contains but one house ;—there
    I lost you.

BLOUNT.

One house !

BELLAIR.

Where a widow named Vizard——

BLOUNT (*aside*).

                      I tremble.

Yes——

BELLAIR.

Resides with an angel——

BLOUNT (*aside*).

       'Twere best to dissemble.
With an angel! bah! say with a girl—what's her
name?

BELLAIR.

On this earth, Lucy Wilmot.

BLOUNT.

       Eh!—Wilmot?

BELLAIR.

       The same.

BLOUNT (*after a short pause*).

And how knew you these ladies?

BELLAIR.

       Will you be my friend?

BLOUNT.

I? of course.   Tell me all from beginning to end.

BELLAIR.

Oh, my story is short.   Just a fortnight ago,
Coming home tow'rds the night from my club——

BLOUNT.

Drunk?

BELLAIR.

So, so.

"Help me, help!" cries a voice—'tis a woman's—
    I run—
Which may prove I'd drunk less than I often have
    done.
And I find—but, dear Blount, you have heard the
    renown
Of a set called the Mohawks?

BLOUNT.

                The scourge of the town.

A lewd band of night savages, scouring the street,
Sword in hand,—and the terror of all whom they
    meet
Not as bad as themselves;—*you* were safe, sir;
    proceed.

BELLAIR.

In the midst of the Mohawks I saw her and
    freed——

BLOUNT.

You saw *her*—Lucy Wilmot—at night, and alone?

BELLAIR.

No, she had a protector—the face of that crone.

BLOUNT.

Mistress Vizard?

BELLAIR.

      The same, yet, tho' strange it appear,
When the rogues saw her face they did *not* fly in
    fear.
Brief—I came, saw, and conquered—but own, on
    the whole,
That my conquest was helped by the City Patrol.
I escorted them home—at their threshold we part—
And I mourn since that night for the loss of my
    heart.

BLOUNT.

Did you call the next day to demand back that
    treasure?

BELLAIR.

Yes.

BLOUNT.

And saw the young lady ?

BELLAIR.

     I had not that pleasure ;
I saw the old widow, who told me politely
That her house was too quiet for visits so sprightly ;
That young females brought up in the school of
  propriety
Must regard all young males as the pests of
  society.
I will spare you her lectures, she showed me the
  door,
And closed it.

BLOUNT.

  You've seen Lucy Wilmot no more ?

BELLAIR.

Pardon, yes—very often ; that is, once a-day.
Every house has its windows——

BLOUNT.

     Ah ! what did you say ?

BELLAIR.

Well, by words very little, but much by the eyes.
Now instruct me in turn,—from what part of the
  skies
Did my angel descend? What her parents and race?
She is well-born, no doubt—one sees *that* in her face.
What to her is Dame Vizard—that awful duenna,
With the look of a griffiness fed upon senna?
Tell me all. Ho there!—drawer, a pottle of clary!

BLOUNT.

Leave in peace the poor girl whom you never could
  marry.

BELLAIR.

Why?

BLOUNT.

Her station's too mean. In a small country
  town
Her poor mother taught music.

BELLAIR.

Her father?
(DRAWER *places wine and glasses on the
  table.*)

BLOUNT.

Unknown.
From the mother's deathbed, from the evil and
    danger
That might threaten her youth, she was brought
    by a stranger
To the house of the lady who——

BELLAIR.

Showed me the door?

BLOUNT.

Till instructed to live, like her mother before,
As a teacher of music. My noble young friend,
To a match so unmeet you could never descend.
You assure me, I trust, that all thought is dismist
Of a love so misplaced.

BELLAIR.

No *(filling* BLOUNT's *glass)*—her health!

BLOUNT.

You persist?
Dare you, sir, to a man of my tenets austere,

Ev'n to hint your designs if your suit persevere ?
What !—you still would besiege her ?

BELLAIR.

Of course, if I love.

BLOUNT.

I am Virtue's defender, sir—there is my glove.
(*Flings down his glove, and rises in angry
excitement.*)

BELLAIR.

Noble heart ! I esteem you still more for this heat.
In the list of my sins there's no room for deceit ;
And to plot against innocence helpless and weak—
I'd as soon pick a pocket !

BLOUNT.

What mean you then ? Speak.

BELLAIR.

Blount, I mean you to grant me the favour I ask.

BLOUNT.

What is that ?

BELLAIR.

To yourself an agreeable task.
Since you know this Dame Vizard, you call there
   to-day,
And to her and to Lucy say all I would say.
You attest what I am—fortune, quality, birth,
Adding all that your friendship allows me of worth.
Blount, I have not a father; I claim you as one;
You will plead for my bride as you'd speak for a son.
All arranged—to the altar we go in your carriage,
And I'll vote as you wish the month after my
   marriage.

BLOUNT (*aside*).

Can I stifle my fury?

Enter NEWSMAN *with papers.*

NEWSMAN.

Great news!

BELLAIR.

Silence, ape!
(*Coffee-house loungers rise and crowd round
   the* NEWSMAN—VEASEY *snatching the
   paper.*)

OMNES.

Read.

VEASEY (*reading*).

" Lord Nithsdale, the rebel, has made his escape.
His wife, by permission of Walpole last night,
Saw her lord in the Tower——— "

(*Great sensation.*)

BELLAIR (*to* BLOUNT).

You will make it all right.

VEASEY (*continuing*).

" And the traitor escaped in her mantle and dress."

BELLAIR (*to* BLOUNT).

Now my fate's in your hands—I may count on you.

BLOUNT.

Yes.

END OF ACT I.

ACT SECOND.

SCENE I.

A room in WALPOLE'S *house. Pictures on the wall. A large table with books, papers, &c.*

WALPOLE *and* VEASEY *seated.*

WALPOLE.

And so Nithsdale's escaped ! His wife's mantle and
    gown ;
Well—ha, ha! let us hope he's now out of this
    town,
And in safer disguise than my lady's attire,
Gliding fast down the Thames—which he'll not set
    on fire.

VEASEY.

All your colleagues are furious.

WALPOLE.

Ah yes; if they catch him,
Not a hand from the crown of the martyr could
    snatch him !
Of a martyr so pitied the troublesome ghost
Would do more for his cause than the arms of a
    host.
These reports from our agents, in boro' and shire,
Show how slowly the sparks of red embers expire.
Ah ! what thousands will hail in a general election
The wild turbulent signal for——

VEASEY.

Fresh insurrection.

WALPOLE (*gravely*).

Worse than that ;—Civil War !—at all risk, at all
    cost,
We must carry this bill, or the nation is lost.

VEASEY.

Will not Tory and Roundhead against it unite ?

WALPOLE.

Every man has his price; I must bribe left and
 right.
So you've failed with Bellair—a fresh bait we must
 try.
As for Blount——

Enter SERVANT.

SERVANT.

Mr Blount.

WALPOLE.

Pray admit him. Good-bye.
(*Exit* VEASEY).

SCENE II.

WALPOLE, BLOUNT.

BLOUNT.

Mr Walpole, you ask my advice on the dues
Which the City imposes on coal.

WALPOLE.

                                  Sir, excuse
That pretence for some talk on more weighty a
    theme,
With a man who commands——

BLOUNT (*aside*).

                                  Forty votes.

WALPOLE.

                                  My esteem.
You're a patriot, and therefore I courted this visit.
Hark! your country's in danger—great danger,
    sir.

BLOUNT (*drily*).

                                  Is it?

WALPOLE.

And I ask you to save it from certain perdition.

BLOUNT.

Me!—I am——

WALPOLE.

Yes, at present in hot opposition.

But what's party ? Mere cricket—some out and
some in ;

I have been out myself. At that time I was thin,

Atrabilious, sir—jaundiced ; now, rosy and stout,

Nothing pulls down a statesman like long fagging
out.

And to come to the point, now there's nobody by,

Be as stout and as rosy, dear Selden, as I.

What! when bad men conspire, shall not good men
combine ?

There's a place—the Paymastership—just in your
line ;

I may say that the fees are ten thousand a-year,

Besides extras—not mentioned. (*Aside.*) The rogue
will cost dear.

BLOUNT.

What has that, sir, to do with the national danger

To which——

WALPOLE.

You're too wise to be wholly a stranger.

Need I name to a man of your Protestant true
heart
All the risks we yet run from the Pope and the
Stuart?
And the indolent public is so unenlightened
That 'tis not to be trusted, and scarce to be fright-
ened.
When the term of this Parliament draws to its close,
Should King George call another, 'tis filled with
his foes.

BLOUNT.

You pay soldiers eno' if the Jacobites rise——

WALPOLE.

But a Jacobite house would soon stop their sup-
plies.
There's a General, on whom you must own, on
reflection,
The Pretender relies.

BLOUNT.
Who?

WALPOLE.
The General Election.

BLOUNT.

That election must come ; you have no other choice.
Would you juggle the People and stifle its voice ?

WALPOLE.

That is just what young men fresh from college
  would say,
And the People's a very good thing in its way.
But what is the People ?—the mere population ?
No, the sound-thinking part of this practical nation,
Who support peace and order, and steadily all poll
For the weal of the land !

BLOUNT (*aside*).

In plain words, for Bob Walpole.

WALPOLE.

Of a people like this I've no doubts nor mistrustings,
But I have of the fools who vote wrong at the
  hustings.
Sir, in short, I am always frank-spoken and hearty,
England needs all the patriots that go with your
  party.

We must make the three years of this Parliament
    seven,
And stave off Civil War.   You agree?

BLOUNT.

                   Gracious heaven!
Thus to silence the nation, to baffle its laws,
And expect Selden Blount to defend such a cause!
What could ever atone for so foul a disgrace?

WALPOLE.

Everlasting renown—(*aside*) and the Paymaster's
    place.

BLOUNT.

Sir, your servant—good day; I am not what you
    thought;
I am honest——

WALPOLE.

Who doubts it?

BLOUNT.

                And not to be bought.

WALPOLE.

You are not to be bought, sir—astonishing man !
Let us argue that point.   If creation you scan,
You will find that the children of Adam prevail
O'er the beasts of the field but by barter and sale.
Talk of coals—if it were not for buying and
    selling,
Could you coax from Newcastle a coal to your
    dwelling ?
You would be to your own fellow-men good for
    nought,
Were it true, as you say, that you're not to be
    bought.
If you find men worth nothing—say, don't you
    despise them ?
And what proves them worth nothing ?—why,
    nobody buys them.
But a man of such worth as yourself ! nonsense—
    come,
Sir, to business ; I want you—I buy you ; the sum ?

BLOUNT.

Is corruption so brazen ? are manners so base ?

WALPOLE (*aside*).

That means he don't much like the Paymaster's
place.

(*With earnestness and dignity.*)

Pardon, Blount, I spoke lightly ; but do not mistake,—

On mine honour, the peace of the land is at stake.

Yes, the peace and the freedom !   Were Hampden
himself

Living still, would he side with the Stuart or Guelph ?

When the Cæsars the freedom of Rome overthrew,

All its forms they maintained—'twas its spirit
they slew !

Shall the freedom of England go down to the
grave ?

No ! the forms let us scorn, so the spirit we save.

BLOUNT.

England's peace and her freedom depend on your
bill ?

WALPOLE (*seriously*).

Thou know'st it—and therefore——

BLOUNT.

My aid you ask still ?

WALPOLE. .

Nay, no longer *I* ask, 'tis thy country petitions.

BLOUNT.

But you talked about terms.

WALPOLE (*pushing pen and paper to him*).

There, then, write your conditions.
(BLOUNT *writes, folds the paper, gives it
to* WALPOLE, *bows, and exit.*)

WALPOLE (*reading*).

" 'Mongst the men who are bought to save Eng-
land inscribe me,
And my bribe is the head of the man who would
bribe me."
Eh! my head! That ambition is much too high-
reaching;
I suspect that the crocodile hints at impeaching.
And he calls himself honest ! What highwayman's
worse ?—
Thus to threaten my life when I offer my purse.

Hem ! he can't be in debt, as the common talk runs,
For the man who scorns money has never known
  duns.
And yet *have* him I must ! Shall I force or entice ?
Let me think—let me think ; every man has his
  price.

(Exit W<small>ALPOLE</small>.)

SCENE III.

A room in M<small>RS</small> V<small>IZARD</small>'s *house. At the back a
large window opening on a balcony. In
one angle of the room a small door, concealed in the wainscoting. In another
angle folding-doors, through which the visi-
tors enter. At each of the side scenes in
front, another door.*

Enter M<small>RS</small> V<small>IZARD</small>.

MRS VIZARD.

'Tis the day when the Jacobite nobles bespeak
This safe room for a chat on affairs once a-week.

(Knock without.)

Ah, they come.

Enter two JACOBITE LORDS, *and* NITHSDALE
disguised as a woman.

1*st* JACOBITE LORD.

Ma'am, well knowing your zeal for our king,
To your house we have ventured this lady to bring.
She will quit you at sunset—nay, haply, much
    sooner—
For a voyage to France in some trusty Dutch
    schooner.
Hist !—her husband in exile she goes to rejoin,
And our homes are so watched——

MRS VIZARD.

                    That she's safer in mine.
Come with me, my dear lady, I have in my care
A young ward——

1*st* JACOBITE LORD (*hastily*).

            Who must see her not ! Till we prepare
Her departure, conceal her from all prying eyes ;
She is timid, and looks on new faces as spies.
Send your servant on business that keeps her away
Until nightfall ;—her trouble permit me to pay.
                    (*Giving a purse.*)

MRS VIZARD.

Nay, my lord, I don't need——

1st JACOBITE LORD.

Quick—your servant release.

MRS VIZARD.

I will send her to Kent with a note to my niece.
(*Exit* MRS VIZARD.)

1st JACOBITE LORD *to* NITHSDALE.

Here you're safe; still, I tremble until you are
freed;
Keep sharp watch at the window—the signal's
agreed.
When a pebble's thrown up at the pane, you will
know
'Tis my envoy ;—a carriage will wait you below.

NITHSDALE.

And if, ere you can send him, some peril befall?

1st JACOBITE LORD.

Risk your flight to the inn near the steps at
Blackwall.

Re-enter MRS VIZARD.

MRS VIZARD.

She is gone.

1*st* JACOBITE LORD.

Lead the lady at once to her room.

MRS VIZARD (*opening door to right of side scene*).
No man dares enter here.

NITHSDALE (*aside*).

Where she sleeps, I presume.
(*Exeunt* MRS VIZARD *and* NITHSDALE.)

2*d* JACOBITE LORD.

You still firmly believe, tho' revolt is put down,
That King James is as sure to recover his crown.

1*st* JACOBITE LORD.

Yes; but wait till this Parliament's close is decreed,
And then up with our banner from Thames to the
Tweed.
(*Knock at the street-door.*)
Who knocks? Some new friend?

Enter MRS VIZARD.

MRS VIZARD (*looking out of the window*).

　　　Oh! quick—quick—do not stay!
It is Blount.

Both LORDS.

What!—the Roundhead?

MRS VIZARD (*opening concealed door in the angle*).

　　　Here—here—the back way.
　　　　　(*Exit* MRS VIZARD.)

1*st* JACOBITE LORD (*as they get to the door*).

Hush! and wait till he's safe within doors.

2*d* JACOBITE LORD.

　　　　　But our foes
She admits?

1*st* JACOBITE LORD.

By my sanction,—their plans to disclose.
　　(*Exeunt* JACOBITE LORDS *just as enter*
　　　BLOUNT *and* MRS VIZARD.)

SCENE IV.

Mrs Vizard, Blount.

MRS VIZARD.

I had sent out my servant; this is not your hour.

BLOUNT.

Mistress Vizard.

MRS VIZARD.

Sweet sir! (*Aside.*) He looks horridly sour.

BLOUNT.

I enjoined you, when trusting my ward to your
care——

MRS VIZARD.

To conceal from herself the true name that you
bear.

BLOUNT.

And she still has no guess——

MRS VIZARD.

That in Jones, christened John,
'Tis the great Selden Blount whom she gazes upon.

D

BLOUNT.

And my second injunction——

MRS VIZARD.

Was duly to teach her
To respect all you say, as if said by a preacher.

BLOUNT.

A preacher !—not so ; as a man she should rather
Confide in, look up to, and love as——

MRS VIZARD.

A father.

BLOUNT.

Hold ! I did not say " Father." You might, for
    you can,
Call me——

MRS VIZARD.

What ?

BLOUNT.

Hang it, madam, a fine-looking man.
But at once to the truth which your cunning
　　secretes,
How came Lucy and you, ma'am, at night in the
　　streets ?

MRS VIZARD.

I remember. Poor Lucy so begged and so cried—
On that day, a year since——

BLOUNT.
　　　　　　　　　　　Well !

MRS VIZARD.

　　　　　　　　　　Her poor mother died ;
And all her wounds opened, recalling that day :
She insisted—I had not the heart to say nay—
On the solace religion alone can bestow ;
So I led her to church,—does that anger you ?

BLOUNT.
　　　　　　　　　　　　　　No !

But at nightfall——

MRS VIZARD.

I knew that the church would be dark ;
And thus nobody saw us, not even the clerk.

BLOUNT.

And returning——

MRS VIZARD.

We fell into terrible danger.
Sir, the Mohawks——

BLOUNT.

I know ; you were saved by a stranger.
He escorted you home; called the next day, I hear.

MRS VIZARD.

But I soon sent him off with a flea in his ear.

BLOUNT.

Since that day the young villain has seen her.

MRS VIZARD.

Oh no !

BLOUNT.

Yes.

MRS VIZARD.

And where ?

BLOUNT.

At the window.

MRS VIZARD.

You do not say so !

What deceivers girls are ! how all watch they
befool !

One should marry them off, ere one sends them to
school !

BLOUNT.

Ay, I think you are right. All our plans have
miscarried.

Go ; send Lucy to me — it is time she were
married.

(*Exit* Mrs VIZARD *by door to left of side
scene.*)

BLOUNT.

When I first took this orphan, forlorn and alone,

From the poor village inn where I sojourned un-
    known,
My compassion no feeling more sensitive masked.
She was grateful—that pleased me ; was more than
    I asked.
'Twas in kindness I screened myself under false
    names,
For she told me her father had fought for King James;
And, embued in the Jacobite's pestilent error,
In a Roundhead she sees but a bugbear of terror.
And from me, Selden Blount, who invoked our
    free laws
To behead or to hang all who side with that cause,
She would start with a shudder ! O fool ! how above
Human weakness I thought myself ! This, then,
·   is love !
Heavens ! to lose her—resign to another those
    charms !
No, no ! never ! Why yield to such idle alarms ?
What's that fop she has seen scarcely once in a way
To a man like myself, whom she sees every day ?
Mine she must be ! but how !—the world's laughter
    I dread.
Tut ! the world will not know, if in secret we wed.
    (*Enter* LUCY *by door to left of side scene.*)

SCENE V.

BLOUNT, LUCY.

LUCY.

Dear sir, you look pale.   Are you ill ?

BLOUNT.

Ay, what then ?

What am I in your thoughts ?

LUCY.

The most generous of men.
Can you doubt of the orphan's respectful affection,
When she owes ev'n a home to your sainted pro-
tection ?

BLOUNT.

In that home I had hoped for your youth to secure
Safe escape from the perils that threaten the pure ;
But, alas ! where a daughter of Eve is, I fear
That the serpent will still be found close at her ear.

LUCY.

You alarm me !

BLOUNT.

I ought.   Ah, what danger you ran!
You have seen—have conversed with——

LUCY.
Well, well.

BLOUNT.
A young man.

LUCY.

Nay, he is not so frightful, dear sir, as you deem;
If you only but knew him, I'm sure you'd esteem.
He's so civil—so pleasant—the sole thing I fear
Is—heigh-ho! are fine gentlemen always sincere?

BLOUNT.

You are lost if you heed not the words that I say.
Ah! young men are not now what they were in my
    day.
Then their fashion was manhood, their language
    was truth,
And their love was as fresh as a world in its youth;
Now they fawn like a courtier, and fib like his
    flunkeys,
And their hearts are as old as the faces of monkeys.

LUCY.

Ah! you know not Sir Sidney——

BLOUNT.

His nature I do,

For he owned to my friend his designs upon you.

LUCY.

What designs?

BLOUNT.

Of a nature too dreadful to name.

LUCY.

How! His words full of honour——

BLOUNT.

Veiled thoughts full of shame.

Heard you never of wolves in sheep's clothing?
Why weep?

LUCY.

Indeed, sir, he don't look the least like a sheep.

BLOUNT.

No, the sheepskin for clothing much finer he
trucks;

Wolves are nowaday clad not as sheep—but as
bucks.

'Tis a false heart you find where a fine dress you see,
And a lover sincere is a plain man like me.
Dismiss then, dear child, this young beau from your
    mind—
A young beau should be loathed by good young
    womankind.
At the best he's a creature accustomed to roam ;
'Tis at sixty man learns how to value a home.
Idle fancies throng quick at your credulous age,
And their cure is companionship, cheerful, but sage;
So, in future, I'll give you much more of my own.
Weeping still !—I've a heart, and it is not of stone.

LUCY.

Pardon, sir, these vain tears; nor believe that I
    mourn
For a false-hearted——

BLOUNT.

      Coxcomb, who merits but scorn.
We must give you some change—purer air, livelier
    scene—
And your mind will soon win back its temper
    serene.
You must quit this dull court with its shocking
    look-out.

Yes, a cot is the home of contentment, no doubt.
A sweet cot with a garden—walled round—shall
    be ours,
Where our hearts shall unite in the passion—for
    flowers.
Ah! I know a retreat, from all turmoil remote,
In the suburb of Lambeth—soon reached by a boat.
So that every spare moment to business not due
I can give, my sweet Lucy, to rapture and you.

LUCY.

What means he? His words and his looks are
    alarming :
Mr Jones, you're too good!

BLOUNT.

        What!—to find you so charming?
Yes; tho' Fortune has placed my condition above
    you,
Yet Love levels all ranks. Be not startled—I love
    you.
From all dreams less exalted your fancies arouse;
The poor orphan I raise to the rank of my spouse.

LUCY.

What! His spouse! Do I dream?

BLOUNT.

Till that moment arrives,
Train your mind to reflect on the duty of wives.
I must see Mistress Vizard, and all things prepare;
To secure our retreat shall this day be my care.
And—despising the wretch who has caused us such
  sorrow—
Our two lives shall unite in the cottage to-morrow.

LUCY.

Pray excuse me—this talk is so strangely——

BLOUNT.

Delightful!

LUCY (*aside*).

I am faint; I am all of a tremble: how frightful!
(*Exit through side door to left.*)

BLOUNT.

Good; my mind overawes her! From fear love
  will grow,
And by this time to-morrow a fig for the beau.
(*Calling out.*)
Mistress Vizard!

(*Enter* MRS VIZARD.)

SCENE VI.

BLOUNT, MRS VIZARD.

BLOUNT.

Guard well my dear Lucy to-day,
For to-morrow I free you, and bear her away.
I agree with yourself—it is time she were married,
And I only regret that so long I have tarried.
Eno' !—I've proposed.

MRS VIZARD.
She consented?

BLOUNT.
Of course ;
Must a man like myself get a wife, ma'am, by force ?

NEWSMAN (*without, ringing a bell*).
Great news.

MRS VIZARD (*running to the window, listening and
repeating*).
What ! "Lord Nithsdale escaped from the Tower."
(*Nithsdale peeps through the door of his
room.*)
" In his wife's clothes disguised !—the gown grey,
with red flower,

Mantle black, trimmed with ermine." My hearing
    is hard.
Mr Blount, Mr Blount! Do you hear the reward?

BLOUNT.

Yes; a thousand——

MRS VIZARD.

What!—guineas?

BLOUNT.

                Of course; come away.
I go now for the parson—do heed what I say.
       (*Nithsdale shakes his fist at* MRS VIZARD,
        and retreats.)
We shall marry to-morrow—no witness but you;
For the marriage is private. I'm Jones still.
    Adieu!
                   (*Exit* BLOUNT.)

(LUCY *peeps out.*)

MRS VIZARD.

Ha! a thousand gold guineas!
            (*Locks* NITHSDALE'S *door.*)

Re-enter BLOUNT.

Guard closely my treasure.
That's her door; for precaution, just lock it.

MRS VIZARD.

With pleasure.
(*As she shows out* BLOUNT, LUCY *slips forth.*)

LUCY.

Eh! locked up! No, I yet may escape if I hide.
(*Gets behind the window-curtains.*)

Re-enter MRS VIZARD.

MRS VIZARD.

Shall I act on this news? I must quickly decide.
Surely Nithsdale it is! Grey gown, sprigged with
red;
Did not walk like a woman—a stride, not a tread.
(*Locks* LUCY'S *door.*)
Both my lambs are in fold; I'll steal out and in-
quire.
Robert Walpole might make the reward somewhat
higher.
(*Exit* MRS VIZARD.)

LUCY (*looking out from the window*).

She has locked the street-door.   She has gone
  with the key,
And the servant is out.   No escape; woe is me!
How I love him!   And yet I must see him with
  loathing.
Why should wolves be disguised in such beautiful
  clothing?

NITHSDALE (*knocking violently*).

Let me out.   I'll not perish entrapped.   From your
  snare
Thus I break——
> (*Bursts the door, and comes out bran-
> dishing a poker.*)
>> Treacherous hag!

———

SCENE VII.

LUCY, NITHSDALE.

LUCY.

'Tis the wolf.   Spare me; spare!
  (*Kneeling, and hiding her face.*)

NITHSDALE.

She's a witch, and has changed herself!

LUCY.

Do not come near me.

NITHSDALE.

Nay, young lady, look up!

LUCY.

'Tis a woman!

NITHSDALE.

Why fear me?

Perchance, like myself, you're a prisoner?

LUCY.

Ah yes!

NITHSDALE.

And your kinsfolk are true to the Stuart, I guess.

LUCY.

My poor father took arms for King James.

NITHSDALE.

So did I.

E

LUCY.

You !—a woman !   How brave !

NITHSDALE.

           For that crime I must die
If you will not assist me.

LUCY.

         Assist you—how ?   Say.

NITHSDALE.

That she-Judas will sell me, and goes to betray.

LUCY.

Fly ! Alas ! she has locked the street-door !

NITHSDALE.

           Lady fair,
Does not Love laugh at locksmiths ?   Well, so
    does Despair !

         (*Glancing at the window.*)

Flight is here.   But this dress my detection en-
    sures.
If I could but exchange hood and mantle for
    yours !
Dare I ask you to save me ?

LUCY.

Nay, doubt not my will;
But my own door is locked.

NITHSDALE (*raising the poker*).

And the key is *here* still.
(*Bursts the door of* LUCY's *room and enters.*)

LUCY.

I have read of the Amazons; this must be one.

NITHSDALE (*coming from the door with hood,
gown, and mantle on his arm*).

I have found all I need for the risk I must run.

LUCY.

Can I help you?

NITHSDALE.

Heaven bless thee, sweet Innocence, no.
Haste, and look if no back way is open below.
Stay; your father has served the king over the
water;

And this locket may please your brave father's
    true daughter—.
The grey hair of poor Charles, intertwined with
    the pearl.
Go ; vouchsafe me this kiss.
        (*Kissing her hand, and exit within the door.*)

LUCY.
                    What a wonderful girl !

SCENE VIII.

The exterior of MRS VIZARD'S *house.   Large
    window.   Balcony, area rails below.   A
    court.   Dead walls for side scenes, with
    blue posts at each end, through which the
    actors enter.*

Enter BLOUNT.

BLOUNT.
For the curse of celebrity nothing atones.
The sharp parson I call on, as simple John Jones,

Has no sooner set eyes on my popular front,
Than he cries, " Ha! the Patriot, the great Selden
　　Blount! "
Mistress Vizard must hunt up some priest just
　　from Cam,
Who may gaze on these features, nor guess who I am.
　　　　　　　　　　　　　　　　(*Knocks.*)
Not at home.　Servant out too!　Ah! gone forth,
　　I guess,
To enchant the young bride with a new wedding-
　　dress.
I must search for a parson myself.

　　　(*Enter* BELLAIR *from the opposite side.*)

　　　　　　　　　————

SCENE IX.

BLOUNT, BELLAIR.

BELLAIR (*slapping him on the shoulder*).

　　　　　　　　Blount, your news ?

BLOUNT.

You! and here, sir!　What means——

BELLAIR.

My impatience excuse.
You have seen her ?

BLOUNT.

I have.

BELLAIR.

And have pleaded my cause ;
And of course she consents, for she loves me ?
You pause.

BLOUNT.

Nay, alas ! my dear friend——

BELLAIR.

Speak, and tell me my fate.

BLOUNT.

Quick and rash though your wooing be, it is too
    late ;
She has promised her hand to another.   Bear up !

BELLAIR.

There is many a slip 'twixt the lip and the cup.
Ah ! my rival I'll fight.   Say his name if you
    can.

BLOUNT.

Mr Jones. I am told he's a fine-looking man.

BELLAIR.

His address ?

BLOUNT.

Wherefore ask ? You kill *her* in this duel—
Slay the choice of her heart !

BELLAIR.

Of her heart ; you are cruel.
But if so, why, heaven bless her !

BLOUNT.

My arm—come away !

BELLAIR.

No, my carriage waits yonder. I thank you.
Good day.

(*Exit.*)

BLOUNT.

He is gone ; I am safe—(*shaking his left hand with
his right*) wish you joy, my dear Jones !

(*Exit.*)

(NITHSDALE, *disguised in* LUCY'S *dress
and mantle, opens the window.*)

NITHSDALE.

All is still. How to jump without breaking my
    bones ?

> *(Trying to flatten his petticoats, and with
> one leg over the balcony.)*

Curse these petticoats! Heaven, out of all my
    lost riches,
Why couldst thou not save me one thin pair of
    breeches !
Steps !

> *(Gets back—shuts the window.)*

Re-enter BELLAIR.

> But Blount may be wrong. From her
> own lips alone

Will I learn.

> *(Looking up at the window.)*
> I see some one ; I'll venture this stone.

(Picks up, and throws, a pebble at the window.)

NITHSDALE (*opening the window*).

Joy !—the signal !

SCENE X.

BELLAIR, NITHSDALE.

BELLAIR.

'Tis you ; say my friend was deceived.
(NITHSDALE *makes an affirmative sign.*)
You were snared into——

NITHSDALE.

Hush !

BELLAIR.

Could you guess how I grieved !
But oh! fly from this jail ; I'm still full of alarms.
I've a carriage at hand : trust yourself to these
arms.

(NITHSDALE *tucks up his petticoats, gets
down the balcony backwards, setting
his foot on the area rail.*)

BELLAIR.

Powers above !—what a leg !

(LORD NITHSDALE *turns round on the*
rail, rejects BELLAIR'S *hand, and*
jumps down.)

BELLAIR.

O my charmer! one kiss.

NITHSDALE.

Are you out of your senses?

BELLAIR (*trying to pull up her hood*).

With rapture!

NITHSDALE (*striking him*).

Take this.

BELLAIR.

What a fist! If it hits one so hard before marriage,
What *would* it do after?

NITHSDALE.

Quick—where is the carriage?
Now, sir, give me your hand.

BELLAIR.

I'll be hanged if I do
Till I snatch my first kiss!
(*Lifts the hood and recoils astounded.*)

Who the devil are you?
(NITHSDALE *tries to get from him. A*
struggle. BELLAIR *prevails.*)

BELLAIR.

I will give you in charge, or this moment confess
How you pass as my Lucy, and wear her own dress?

NITHSDALE (*aside*).

What! His Lucy? I'm saved.
                                        To her pity I owe
This last chance for my life; would you sell it, sir?

BELLAIR.

                                                    No.
But your life! What's your name? Mine is
    Sidney Bellair.

NITHSDALE.

Who in Parliament pleaded so nobly to spare
From the axe——

BELLAIR.

The chiefs doomed in the Jacobite rise?

NITHSDALE (*with dignity*).

I am Nithsdale. Quick—sell me or free me—time
  flies.

BELLAIR.

Come this way. There's my coach: I will take
  you myself
Where you will ;—ship you off.

NITHSDALE.

Do you side with the Guelph?

BELLAIR.

Yes. What then ?

NITHSDALE.

You would risk your own life by his laws,
Did you ship me to France. They who fight in a
  cause
Should alone share its perils. Farewell, generous
  stranger !

BELLAIR.

Pooh! no gentleman leaves a young lady in danger;
You'd be mobbed ere you got half a yard through
  the town ;

Why, that stride and that calf—let me settle your
    gown.
    (*Clinging to him, and half spoken without.*)
No, no ; I will see you at least to my carriage.
                        (*Behind scene.*)
To what place shall it drive ?

NITHSDALE.
               To Blackwall.

Enter LUCY *from the window.*
                   Hateful marriage !
But where's that poor lady ?   What !—gone ?   She
    is free !
Could she leap from the window ?   I wish I were
    she.   (*Retreats.*)

SCENE XI.

BELLAIR, LUCY.

BELLAIR.
Now she's safe in my coach, on condition, I own,
Not flattering, sweet creature, to leave her alone.

LUCY (*peeping*).

It is he.

BELLAIR.

Ah ! if Lucy would only appear !
(*Stoops to pick up a stone, and in the act
to fling as* LUCY *comes out.*)
O my Lucy !—mine angel !

LUCY.

Why is he so dear ?

BELLAIR.

Is it true?   From that face am I evermore banished?
In your love was the dream of my life! Is it
    vanished ?
Have you pledged to another your hand and your
    heart ?

LUCY.

Not my heart.   Oh, not that.

BELLAIR.

But your hand ?   By what art,
By what force, are you won heart and hand to
    dissever,

And consent to loathed nuptials that part us for
  ever ?

LUCY.

Would that pain you so much ?

BELLAIR.

          Can you ask ?   Oh, believe me,
You're my all in the world !

LUCY.

          I am told you deceive me ;
That you harbour designs which my lips dare not
  name,
And your words full of honour veil thoughts full of
  shame.
Ah, sir ! I'm so young and so friendless—so weak !
Do not ask for my heart if you take it to break.

BELLAIR.

Who can slander me thus ?   Not my friend, I am
  sure.

LUCY.

His friend !

BELLAIR.

Can my love know one feeling impure
When I lay at your feet all I have in this life—
Wealth and rank, name and honour—and woo you
    as wife ?

LUCY.

As your wife ! All about you seems so much above
My mean lot——

BELLAIR.

        And so worthless compared to your love.
You reject, then, this suitor ?—my hand you accept ?

LUCY.

Ah ! but do you not see in what prison I'm kept ?
And this suitor——

BELLAIR.

You hate him !

LUCY.

    Till this day, say rather——

BELLAIR.

What ?

LUCY.

I loved him.

BELLAIR.

You loved !

LUCY.

As I might a grandfather.
He has shielded the orphan ;—I had not a notion
That he claimed from me more than a grandchild's
devotion !
And my heart ceased to beat between terror and
sorrow
When he said he would make me his wife, and to-
morrow.

BELLAIR.

Fly with me, and at once !

LUCY.

She has locked the street-door.

BELLAIR.

And my angel's not made to jump down from that
floor.

F

Listen—quick; I hear voices:—I save you; this
    night
I arrange all we need both for wedlock and flight.
At what time after dark does your she-dragon close
Her sweet eyes, and her household consign to repose?

LUCY.

About nine in this season of winter.   What then?

BELLAIR.

By the window keep watch.   When the clock has
    struck ten
A slight stone smites the casement;—below I attend.
You will see a safe ladder; at once you descend.
We then reach your new home, priest and friends
    shall be there,
Proud to bless the young bride of Sir Sidney Bellair.
Hush! the steps come this way; do not fail!   She
    is won.

                         (*Exit* BELLAIR.)

LUCY.

Stay;—I tremble as guilty.   Heavens! what have
    I done?

END OF ACT II.

ACT THIRD.

SCENE 1.

St James's Park.   Seats, &c.
Time—Sunset.

Enter BLOUNT.

BLOUNT.

So the parson is found and the cottage is hired—
Every fear was dispelled when my rival retired.
Ev'n my stern mother country must spare from my
    life
A brief moon of that honey one tastes with a wife !
And then strong as a giant, recruited by sleep,
On corruption and Walpole my fury shall sweep.
'Mid the cheers of the House I will state in my
    place
How the bribes that he proffered were flung in his
    face.
Men shall class me amid those examples of worth
Which, alas ! become daily more rare on this earth ;

And Posterity, setting its brand on the front
Of a Walpole, select for its homage a Blount.

(*Enter* BELLAIR, *singing gaily.*)

SCENE II.

BLOUNT, BELLAIR.

BELLAIR.

"The dove builds where the leaves are still green
on the tree——"

BLOUNT (*rising*).

Ha!

BELLAIR.

"For May and December can never agree."

BLOUNT.

I am glad you've so quickly got over that blow.

BELLAIR.

Fallala!

BLOUNT (*aside*).

What this levity means I must know.
The friend I best loved was your father, Bellair—
Let me hope your strange mirth is no laugh of
despair.

BELLAIR.

On the wit of the wisest man it is no stigma
If the heart of a girl is to him an enigma;
That my Lucy was lost to my arms you believed—
Wish me joy, my dear Blount, you were grossly
 deceived.
She is mine!—What on earth are you thinking
 about?
Do you hear?

BLOUNT.

I am racked!

BELLAIR.

What?

BLOUNT.

A twinge of the gout.
(*Reseating himself.*)

Pray excuse me.

BELLAIR.

Nay, rather myself I reproach
For not heeding your pain. Let me call you a
 coach.

BLOUNT.

Nay, nay, it is gone.   I am eager to hear
How I've been thus deceived—make my blunder
    more clear.
You have seen her?

BELLAIR.

        Of course.   From her own lips I gather
That your good Mr Jones might be Lucy's
    grandfather.
Childish fear, or of Vizard—who seems a virago—
Or the old man himself——

BLOUNT.
        Oh!

BELLAIR.
        You groan?

BLOUNT.
                The lumbago!

BELLAIR.

Ah! they say gout is shifty—now here and now
    there.

BLOUNT.

Pooh ;—continue. The girl then——

BELLAIR.

I found in despair.
But no matter—all's happily settled at last.

BLOUNT.

Ah ! eloped from the house ?

BELLAIR.

No, the door was made fast.
But to-night I would ask you a favour.

BLOUNT.

What ? Say.

BELLAIR.

If your pain should have left you, to give her away.
For myself it is meet that I take every care
That my kinsfolk shall hail the new Lady Bellair.
I've induced my two aunts (who are prudish) to
    grace
With their presence my house, where the nuptials
    take place.

And to act as her father there's no man so fit
As yourself, dear old Blount, if the gout will permit.

BLOUNT.

'Tis an honour—

BELLAIR.

Say pleasure.

BLOUNT.

Great pleasure!   Proceed.
How is *she,* if the door is still fast, to be freed?
Is the house to be stormed?

BELLAIR.

Nay; I told you before
That a house has its windows as well as its door.
And a stone at the pane for a signal suffices,
While a ladder——

BLOUNT.

I see.   (*Aside.*) What infernal devices!
Has she no maiden fear——

BELLAIR.

From the ladder to fall?
Ask her that—when we meet at my house in
Whitehall.

(*Enter* 1*st* JACOBITE LORD.)

SCENE III.

BLOUNT, BELLAIR, 1*st* JACOBITE, *afterwards* VEASEY.

JACOBITE LORD (*giving note to* BELLAIR).

If I err not, I speak to Sir Sidney Bellair?
Pray vouchsafe me one moment in private.

(*Draws him aside.*)

BLOUNT.

Despair!
How prevent?—how forestall? Could I win but
delay,
I might yet brush this stinging fly out of my way.

(*While he speaks, enter* VEASEY *in the
background.*)

VEASEY.

Ha! Bellair whispering close with that Jacobite
　　lord—
Are they hatching some plot?

　　　　　　(*Hides behind the trees—listening.*)

BELLAIR (*reading*).

　　　　So he's safely on board——

JACOBITE LORD.

And should Fortune shake out other lots from her
　　urn,
We, poor friends of the Stuart, might serve you in
　　turn.
You were talking with Blount—Selden Blount—is
　　he one
Of your friends?

BELLAIR.

Ay, the truest.

JACOBITE LORD.

　　　　　　Then warn him to shun
That vile Jezabel's man-trap—I know he goes there.
Whom she welcomes she sells.

BELLAIR.

I will bid him beware.

(*Shakes hands.* *Exit* JACOBITE LORD.)

BELLAIR (*to* BLOUNT).

I have just learned a secret, 'tis fit I should tell
 you.

Go no more to old Vizard's, or know she will sell
 you.

Nithsdale hid in her house when the scaffold he fled.

She received him, and went for the price on his
 head ;

But—the drollest mistake—of that tale by-and-by—

He was freed ; is safe now !

BLOUNT.

Who delivered him ?

BELLAIR.

I.

BLOUNT.

Ha !—you did !

BELLAIR.

See, he sends me this letter of thanks.

BLOUNT (*reading*).

Which invites you to join with the Jacobite ranks.
And when James has his kingdom——

BELLAIR.

That chance is remote ;

BLOUNT.

Hints an earldom for you.

BELLAIR.

Bah !

BLOUNT.

Take care of this note.
(*Appears to thrust it into* BELLAIR'S
*coat-pocket—lets it fall, and puts
his foot on it.*)

BELLAIR.

Had I guessed that the hag was so greedy of gold,
Long ago I had bought Lucy out of her hold ;
But to-night the dear child will be free from her
power.
Adieu ! I expect you then.

BLOUNT.

Hold! at what hour?

BELLAIR.

By the window at ten, self and ladder await her;
The wedding—eleven; you will not be later.

(*Exit.*)

BLOUNT (*picking up the letter*).

Nithsdale's letter. Bright thought!—and what
luck! I see Veasey.

Re-enter BELLAIR.

BELLAIR.

Blount, I say, will old Jones be to-morrow uneasy?
Can't you fancy his face?

BLOUNT.

Yes; ha! ha!

BELLAIR.

I am off.

(*Exit.*)

SCENE IV.

BLOUNT, VEASEY.

BLOUNT.

What! shall I, Selden Blount, be a popinjay's scoff?
Mr Veasey, your servant.

VEASEY.

　　　　　　　　I trust, on the whole,
That you've settled with Walpole the prices of
　coal.

BLOUNT.

Coals be—lighted below! Sir, the country's in
　danger.

VEASEY.

To that fact Walpole says that no patriot's a
　stranger.

BLOUNT.

With the safety of England myself I will task,
If you hold yourself licensed to grant what I ask.

VEASEY.

Whatsoever the terms of a patriot so stanch,
Walpole gives you—I speak as his proxy—*carte
blanche.*

BLOUNT.

If I break private ties where the Public's at stake,
Still my friend is my friend : the condition I make
Is to keep him shut up from all share in rash strife,
And secure him from danger to fortune and life.

VEASEY.

Blount—agreed. And this friend ? Scarce a moment ago
I marked Sidney Bellair in close talk with——

BLOUNT.
I know.
There's a plot to be checked ere it start into shape.
Hark ! Bellair had a hand in Lord Nithsdale's
escape !

VEASEY.

That's abetment of treason.

BLOUNT.

Read this, and attend.
(*Gives* NITHSDALE'S *note to* BELLAIR,
which VEASEY *reads.*)
Snares atrocious are set to entrap my poor friend
In an outbreak to follow that Jacobite's flight——

VEASEY.

In an outbreak.   Where ?—when ?

BLOUNT.

Hush ! in London to-night.
He is thoughtless and young.   Act on this infor-
mation.
Quick—arrest him at once ; and watch over the
nation.

VEASEY.

No precaution too great against men disaffected.

BLOUNT.

And the law gives you leave to confine the
suspected.

VEASEY.

Ay, this note will suffice for a warrant. Be sure,
Erc the clock strike the quarter, your friend is
  secure.

(*Exit* VEASEY.)

BLOUNT.

Good; my rival to-night will be swept from my
  way,
And John Jones shall wake easy eno' the next day.
Do I still love this girl? No, my hate is so strong,
That to me, whom she mocks, she alone shall
  belong.
I need trust to that saleable Vizard no more.
Ha! I stand as Bellair the bride's window before.
Oh, when love comes so late how it maddens the
  brain,
Between shame for our folly, and rage at our pain!

(*Exit.*)

SCENE V.

Room in WALPOLE'S *house.*   (*Lights.*)

Enter WALPOLE.

So Lord Nithsdale's shipped off.   There's an end
    of one trouble ;
When his head's at Boulogne the reward shall be
    double.

        (*Seating himself, takes up a book —*
           glances at it, and throws it down.)

Stuff !   I wonder what lies the Historians will tell
When they babble of one Robert Walpole !   Well,
    well,
Let them sneer at his blunders, declaim on his
    vices,
Cite the rogues whom he purchased, and rail at
    the prices,
They shall own that all lust for revenge he with-
    stood ;
And, if lavish of gold, he was sparing of blood ;
That when England was threatened by France and
    by Rome,

He forced Peace from abroad and encamped her at
    home,
And the Freedom he left, rooted firm in mild laws,
May o'ershadow the faults of deeds done in her
    cause !

                     (*Enter* VEASEY.)

SCENE VI.

WALPOLE, VEASEY.

VEASEY (*giving note*).

Famous news ! See, Bellair has delivered himself
To your hands. He must go heart and soul with
    the Guelph,
And vote straight, or he's ruined.

WALPOLE (*reading*).

                  This note makes it clear
That he's guilty of Nithsdale's escape.

VEASEY.

                     And I hear
That to-night he will head some tumultuous revolt,
Unless chained to his stall like a mischievous colt.

WALPOLE.

Your informant ?

VEASEY.

Guess ! Blount; but on promise to save
His young friend's life and fortune !

WALPOLE.

What Blount says is grave.
He would never thus speak if not sure of his fact.
(*Signing warrant.*)
Here, then, take my State warrant; but cautiously
act.
Bid Bellair keep his house — forbid exits and
entries ;—
To make sure, at his door place a couple of
sentries.
Say I mean him no ill; but these times will excuse
Much less gentle precautions than those which I
use.
Stay, Dame Vizard is waiting without : to her den
Nithsdale fled. She came here to betray him.

VEASEY.

What then ?

WALPOLE.

Why, I kept her, perforce, till I sent, on the sly,
To prevent her from hearing Lord Nithsdale's
 good-bye.
When my agent arrived, I'm delighted to say
That the cage-wires were broken,—the bird flown
 away ;
But he found one poor captive imprisoned and
 weeping ;
I must learn how that captive came into such
 keeping.
Now, then, off—nay, a moment ; you would not be
 loth
Just to stay with Bellair ?—I may send for you both.

VEASEY.

With a host more delightful no mortal could sup,
But a guest so unlooked for——

WALPOLE.

     Will cheer the boy up !
      (*Exit* VEASEY.)

  WALPOLE (*ringing hand-bell*).
      (*Enter* SERVANT.)
Usher in Mistress Vizard.

SCENE VII.

WALPOLE, MRS VIZARD.

WALPOLE.

Quite shocked to detain you,
But I knew a mistake, if there were one, would pain
you.

MRS VIZARD.

Sir, mistake there is not ; that vile creature is no
man.

WALPOLE.

But you locked the door ?

MRS VIZARD.

Fast.

WALPOLE.

Then, no doubt, 'tis a woman,
For she slipped thro' the window.

MRS VIZARD.

No woman durst !

WALPOLE.

Nay.
When did woman want courage to go her own way ?

MRS VIZARD.

You jest, sir.   To me 'tis no subject of laughter.

WALPOLE.

Do not weep.   The reward?—we'll discuss that
hereafter.

MRS VIZARD.

You'd not wrong a poor widow who brought you
such news?

WALPOLE.

Wrong a widow!—there's oil to put in her cruse.
                    (*Giving a pocket-book.*)
Meanwhile, the tried agent despatched to your
house,
In that trap found a poor little terrified mouse,
Which did call itself "Wilmot"—a name known
to me.
Pray you, how in your trap did that mouse come
to be?

MRS VIZARD (*hesitatingly*).

Sir, believe me——

WALPOLE.

Speak truth—for your own sake you ought.

MRS VIZARD.

By a gentleman, sir, to my house she was brought.

WALPOLE.

Oh! some Jacobite kinsman perhaps?

MRS VIZARD.

Bless you, no;
A respectable Roundhead.   You frighten me so!

WALPOLE.

A respectable Roundhead intrust to your care
A young girl, whom you guard as in prison!—
Beware!
'Gainst decoy for vile purpose the law is severe.

MRS VIZARD.

Fie! you libel a saint, sir, of morals austere.

WALPOLE.

Do you mean Judith Vizard?

MRS VIZARD.

I mean Selden Blount.

WALPOLE.

I'm bewildered!   But why does this saint (no affront)
To your pious retreat a fair damsel confide?

MRS VIZARD.

To protect her as ward till he claims her as bride.

WALPOLE.

Faith, his saintship does well until that day arrive
To imprison the maid he proposes to wive.
But these Roundheads are wont but with Round-
 heads to wed,
And the name of this lady is Wilmot, she said.
Every Wilmot I know of is to the backbone
A rank Jacobite; say, can that name be her own?

MRS VIZARD.

Not a doubt; more than once I have heard the
 girl say
That her father had fought for King James on the
 day
When the ranks of the Stuart were crushed at the
 Boyne.
He escaped from the slaughter, and fled to rejoin
At the Court of St Germain's his new-wedded bride.
Long their hearth without prattlers; a year ere he
 died,
Lucy came to console her who mourned him, bereft
Of all else in this world.

WALPOLE (*eagerly*).

But the widow he left;
She lives still ?

MRS VIZARD.

No ; her child is now motherless.

WALPOLE (*aside*).

Fled !
Fled again from us, sister ! How stern are the dead !
Their dumb lips have no pardon !   Tut ! shall I
     build grief
On a guess that perchance only fools my belief ?
This may *not* be her child.   (*Rings*).

(*Enter* SERVANT.)
My coach waits ?

SERVANT.

At the door.

WALPOLE.

Come ; your house teems with secrets I long to
     explore.

(*Exeunt* WALPOLE *and* MRS VIZARD.)

SCENE VIII.

MRS VIZARD'S *house.   A lamp on the table.*

Enter LUCY *from her room.*

LUCY.

Mistress Vizard still out !

(Looking at the clock.)

What! so late ?   O my heart !—

How it beats !   Have I promised in stealth to
   depart ?

Trust him—yes !   But will *he*, ah ! long after this
   night,

Trust the wife wooed so briefly, and won but by
   flight ?

My lost mother !

(Takes a miniature from her breast.)

Oh couldst thou yet counsel thy child !

No, this lip does not smile as it yesterday smiled.

From thine heaven can no warning voice come to
   mine ear ;

Save thy child from herself ;—'tis myself that I
   fear.

Enter WALPOLE *and* MRS VIZARD *through the concealed door.*

MRS VIZARD.

Lucy, love, in this gentleman (curtsy, my dear)
See a friend.

WALPOLE.

Peace, and leave us.

(*Exit* MRS VIZARD.)

———

SCENE IX.

WALPOLE, LUCY.

WALPOLE.

Fair girl, I would hear
From yourself, if your parents——

LUCY.

My parents; Oh say
Did you know them?—my mother?

WALPOLE.

The years roll away.
I behold a grey hall, backed by woodlands of pine;
I behold a fair face—eyes and tresses like thine—

By her side a rude boy full of turbulent life,
All impatient of rest, and all burning for strife—
They are brother and sister. Unconscious they
    stand—
On the spot where their paths shall divide—hand
    in hand.
Hush ! a moment, and lo ! as if lost amid night,
She is gone from his side, she is snatched from his
    sight.
Time has flowed on its course—that wild boy lives
    in me ;
But the sister I lost ! Does she bloom back in
    thee ?
Speak—the name of thy mother, ere changing her
    own
For her lord's ?—who her parents ?

LUCY.
               I never have known.
When she married my father, they spurned her,
    she said,
Bade her hold herself henceforth to them as the
    dead ;
Slandered him in whose honour she gloried as
    wife,

Urged attaint on his name, plotted snares for his
   life;
And one day when I asked what her lineage, she
   sighed
"From the heart they so tortured their memory
   has died."

WALPOLE.

Civil war slays all kindred—all mercy, all ruth.

LUCY.

Did you know her?—if so, was this like her in
   youth?

(*Giving miniature.*)

WALPOLE.

It is she; the lips speak! Oh, I knew it!—thou art
My lost sister restored!—to mine arms, to mine
   heart.
That wild brother the wrongs of his race shall atone;
He has stormed his way up to the foot of the
   throne.
Yes! thy mate thou shalt choose 'mid the chiefs of
   the land.

Dost thou shrink? —heard I right?—is it promised
    this hand,
And to one, too, of years so unsuited to thine?

LUCY.

Dare I tell you?

WALPOLE.

Speak, sure that thy choice shall be mine.

LUCY.

When my mother lay stricken in mind and in
    frame,
All our scant savings gone, to our succour there
    came
A rich stranger, who lodged at the inn whence
    they sought
To expel us as vagrants.   Their mercy he bought;
Ever since I was left in the wide world alone,
I have owed to his pity this roof——

WALPOLE.

                    Will you own
What you gave in return?

LUCY.

Grateful reverence.

WALPOLE.

And so

He asked more !

LUCY.

Ah ! that more was not mine to bestow.

WALPOLE.

What ! your heart some one younger already had
    won.
Is he handsome ?

LUCY.
Oh yes !

WALPOLE.

And a gentleman's son.

LUCY.

Sir, he looks it.

WALPOLE.
His name is—— -

LUCY.

Sir Sidney Bellair.

WALPOLE.

Eh! that brilliant Lothario? Dear Lucy, beware;
Men of temper so light may make love in mere
    sport.
Where on earth did you meet?—in what terms did
    he court?
Why so troubled? Why turn on the timepiece
    your eye?
Orphan, trust me.

LUCY.

I will. I half promised to fly——

WALPOLE.

With Bellair. (*Aside.*) He shall answer for this
    with his life.
Fly to-night as his—what!

LUCY.

Turn your face—as his wife.
(LUCY *sinks down, burying her face in
    her hands.*)

H

WALPOLE (*going to the door*).

Jasper—ho !
  (*Enter* SERVANT *as he writes on his tablets.*)
  Take my coach to Sir Sidney's, Whitehall.
Mr Veasey is there ; give him this—that is all.
   (*Tearing out the leaf from the tablet
   and folding it up.*)
Go out the back way ; it is nearest my carriage.*
   (*Opens the concealed door, through which
   exit* SERVANT.)
I shall very soon know if the puppy means mar-
riage.

LUCY.

Listen ; ah ! that's his signal !

WALPOLE.

     A stone at the pane !
But it can't be Bellair—*he* is safe.

LUCY.
      There, again !

---

* In obeying this instruction, the servant would not see the ladder, which (as the reader will learn by what immediately follows) is
placed against the balcony in the *front* of the house.

WALPOLE (*peeps from the window*).

Ho!—a ladder!   Niece, do as I bid you ; confide
In my word, and I promise Sir Sidney his bride !
Ope the window and whisper, " I'm chained to the
    floor ;
Pray, come up and release me ! "

LUCY (*out of the window*).
                    " I'm chained to the floor ;
Pray, come up and release me."

WALPOLE.
                    I watch by this door.
(*Enters* LUCY's *room and peeping out.*)
(BLOUNT *enters through the window.*)

SCENE X.

BLOUNT, LUCY, WALPOLE *at watch unobserved.*

LUCY.

Saints in heaven, Mr Jones !

WALPOLE (*aside*).
            Selden Blount, by Old Nick !

BLOUNT.

What ! you are not then chained !　Must each word
　　be a trick ?
Ah! you looked for a gallant more dainty and trim ;
He deputes me to say he abandons his whim ;
By his special request I am here in his place—
Saving him from a crime and yourself from dis-
　　grace.
Still, ungrateful, excuse for your folly I make—
Still the prize he disdains to my heart I can take.
Fly with me, as with him you would rashly have
　　fled ;—
He but sought to degrade you, I seek but to wed.
Take revenge on the false heart, give bliss to the
　　true!

LUCY.

If he's false to myself, I were falser to you,
Could I say I forget him ;

BLOUNT.

　　　　　You will, when my wife.

LUCY.

That can never be——

BLOUNT.

Never!

LUCY.

One love lasts thro' life!

BLOUNT.

Traitress! think not this insult can tamely be borne—
Hearts like mine are too proud for submission to
    scorn.
You are here at my mercy—that mercy has died;
You remain as my victim or part as my bride.
                       (*Locks the door.*)
See, escape is in vain, and all others desert you ;
Let these arms be your refuge.

    WALPOLE (*tapping him on the shoulder*).

                    Well said, Public Virtue!
    (BLOUNT, *stupefied, drops the key, which*
        WALPOLE *takes up, stepping out into*
        the balcony, to return as BLOUNT,
        recovering himself, makes a rush at
        the window.)

    WALPOLE (*stopping him*).

As you justly observed, "See, escape is in vain "—
I have pushed down the ladder.

BLOUNT (*laying his hand on his sword*).
　　　　　'Sdeath ! draw, sir !——

WALPOLE.
　　　　　　　　　　　Abstain
From that worst of all blunders, a profitless crime.
Cut my innocent throat ?　Fie ! one sin at a time.

BLOUNT.
Sir, mock on, I deserve it ; expose me to shame,
I've o'erthrown my life's labour,—an honest man's
　　name.

LUCY (*stealing up to* BLOUNT).
No ; a moment of madness can not sweep away
All I owed, and—forgive me—have failed to repay :
　　　　　　　　　　(*To* WALPOLE.)
Be that moment a secret.

WALPOLE.
　　　　　　　　If woman can keep one,
Then a secret's a secret.　Gad, Blount, you're a deep
　　one !
　　　　　(*Knock at the door ;* WALPOLE *opens it.*)

　　　　　(*Enter* BELLAIR *and* VEASEY, *followed by*
　　　　　　　　MRS VIZARD.)

SCENE XI.

WALPOLE, LUCY, BLOUNT, VEASEY, BELLAIR, MRS VIZARD *in the background.*

BELLAIR (*not seeing* WALPOLE, *who is concealed behind the door which he opens, and hurrying to* BLOUNT).

Faithless man, canst thou look on my face undismayed?

Nithsdale's letter disclosed, and my friendship betrayed!

What! and *here* too! Why *here?*

BLOUNT (*aside*).

I shall be the town's scoff.

WALPOLE (*to* BELLAIR *and* VEASEY).

Sirs, methinks that you see not that lady—hats off.

I requested your presence, Sir Sidney Bellair,

To make known what you owe to the friend who stands there.

For that letter disclosed, your harsh language recant—

It's condition your pardon ;—full pardon I grant.
He is here—you ask why ; 'tis to save you to-night
From degrading your bride by the scandal of flight.

(Drawing him aside.)

Or—hist !—*did* you intend (whisper close in my
ear)
Honest wedlock with one so beneath you I fear ?
You of lineage so ancient——

BELLAIR.

Must mean what I say.
Do their ancestors teach the Well-born to betray ?

WALPOLE.

Wed her friendless and penniless ?

BELLAIR.

Ay.

WALPOLE.

Strange caprice !
Deign to ask, then, from Walpole the hand of his
niece.
Should he give his consent, thank the friend you
abuse.

BELLAIR (*embracing* BLOUNT).

Best and noblest of men, my blind fury excuse!

WALPOLE.

Hark! her father's lost lands may yet serve for her
dower.

BELLAIR.

All the earth has no lands worth the bloom of this
flower.

LUCY.

Ah! too soon fades the flower.

BELLAIR.

True, I alter the name.
Be my perfect pure chrysolite—ever the same.

WALPOLE.

Hold! I know not a chrysolite from a carbuncle,
(*With insinuating blandishment of voice
and look.*)
But my nephew-in-law should not vote out his
uncle.

BELLAIR.

Robert Walpole, at last you have bought me, I fear.

WALPOLE.

Every man has his price.   My majority's clear.
If,——
> (*Crossing quickly to Blount.*)
Dear Blount, did your goodness not rank
with the best,
What you feel as reproach, you would treat as a jest.
Raise your head—and with me keep a laugh for
the ass
Who has never gone out of his wits for a lass :
Live again for your country—reflect on my bill.

BLOUNT (*with emotion, grasping* WALPOLE'S *hand*).

You are generous ; I thank you.   Vote *with*
you ?—I will !

VEASEY.

How dispersed arc the clouds seeming lately so
sinister !

WALPOLE.

Yes, I think that the glass stands at Fair—for the
Minister.

VEASEY.

Ah! what more could you do for the People and
Throne?

WALPOLE.

Now I'm safe in my office, I'd leave well alone.

THE END.

PRINTED BY WILLIAM BLACKWOOD AND SONS, EDINBURGH.